SUNDAY
WEEK

Dinah Johnson

illustrated by Tyrone Geter

Henry Holt and Company
New York

 Blue Monday,
everybody's got
the Monday morning blues.

On those
true blue Mondays
the whole neighborhood
has the blues.
The grown-ups don't
want to go to work
and the children don't
want to go to school.
Miss Clara says,
"One day at a time,
sweet Jesus,
that's all I'm asking from you."

The double Dutch champions
of the neighborhood
practice every
Tuesday afternoon,
step step step step,
high high high high,
while people go on
about their business
hurrying here and there.
The champions
keep on keeping on
stepping quick,
stepping high
as the rest of the world
passes by.

Wednesday evenings
Deacon Johnson heads for
choir practice at Lovely Hill
Baptist Church.
Yusef hands out flyers for
a meeting at the mosque.
Desiree lights a candle in the
cathedral and says a prayer
for the people she loves.

Every Thursday, every week,
we sit in a circle
with Miss Augusta,
surrounded by books
filled with magic words.
We can taste them
and hear them
and feel them
and fashion them—
speak words written
and said long ago
to make today
and tomorrow our own.

On Fridays the fishman
cooks for everybody
on the block,
frying brim and catfish
and flounder.
"Just like Jesus
feeding the multitudes,"
Brother Gilliard likes to say.
Hush puppies like loaves,
Kool-Aid in the coolers,
happiness in the hellos,
music in the air.
Finally Friday.

Saturday is workday—
wash those clothes and
hang them out to dry.
Wax the kitchen floor
until it shines.
While you're at it,
wax the car too.
Work and work some more
until there's nothing left to do.
Our mamas don't allow
any work on the seventh day,
so Saturday before we play
we have to get ready
for the Lord's Day.

Come Sunday
come sunrise,
the church bells
make it sound like
heaven is right here.
Come Sunday
come sunrise,
the old folks and
some of the young ones
whisper a little prayer.

Mama's putting
biscuits on the table.
Brother's shining his shoes.
Sister's still memorizing
her Bible verse
while Uncle reads
the morning news.

Come Sunday,
the sidewalks
are a fashion show
everywhere you go.
The women have on fancy hats
and gloves and high heels,
just a-stepping.
Curls are in place,
braids are beaded,
all the boys have gotten
the haircuts they needed.
And all their daddies
are just plain sharp.
They're looking good
when they go to church to be seen,
and to see everybody
they haven't seen all week.

At Lovely Hill
we squirm
on the hard seats
until the church mother
gives us a look that means,
be quiet and listen
to the words
from the Holy Book.
Fans are fanning,
toes are tapping,
coins are clinking
in the offering plate.
The fingers of the organist
do a dance all their own.
The singers in the choir
lift their arms
and in those robes
they look like they mean it
when they sing
"I'll fly away, fly away home."
Reverend Wright
shakes every hand,
calling everybody by name,
saying, "Glad you came."

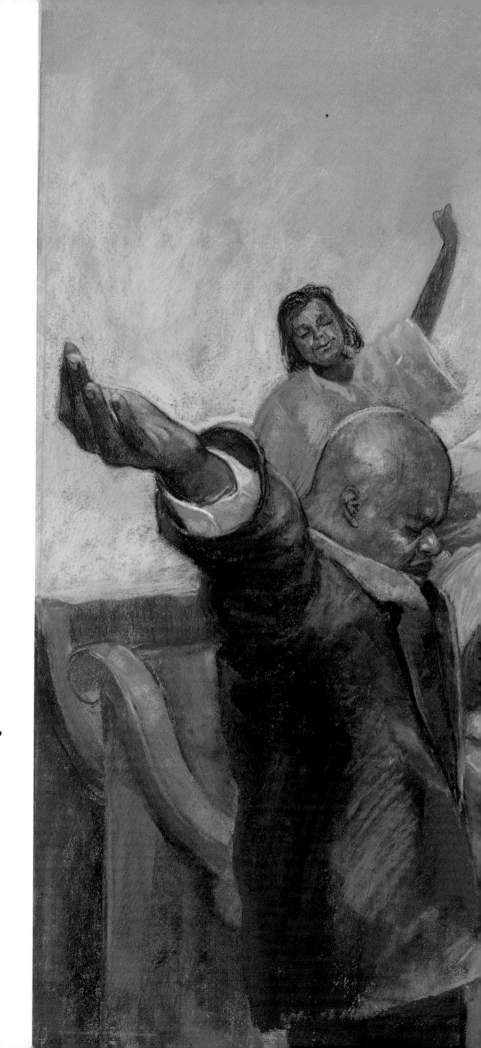

But now he's hungry
like the people
in his congregation
heading home
for Sunday dinner—
food for all God's people,
saints and sinners.
There's fried chicken
coated with Big Mama's
secret recipe.
There's Carolina rice and
black-eyed peas and cornbread
and yams and greens,
just-squeezed lemonade,
and tea and pecan pie.

But today wouldn't be Sunday
without a Sunday drive.
Doesn't matter if you go
near or far
as long as everybody
fits in the car.
Cousins on top of cousins' laps,
with this kind of trip
you don't need a map.
Just go where the road goes
or go where the heart goes
and you'll find yourself
at the home of friends.

 What better way
for the day to end
than with laughter
and just one more slice of pie,
and stories and memories
with the promise of more
afternoons like this to come.

Come Sunday
come sunset,
it's about time to get
on the way back home,
waving God be with you
until we meet again.

Come Sunday . . .

For Frona Johnson and Clara Taylor White, my beloved grandmothers,
and especially for Beatrice Taylor Johnson and Douglas L. Johnson, Sr.,
my extraordinary parents   —D.J.

This book is dedicated to my children, Gerald, Jamila, and Hafizah,
whose love and faith in me has been like a beacon in the deepest, darkest night
that kept me moving toward the light.   —T.G.

Henry Holt and Company, Inc., *Publishers since 1866*, 115 West 18th Street, New York, New York 10011
Henry Holt is a registered trademark of Henry Holt and Company, Inc.

Text copyright © 1999 by Dinah Johnson / Illustrations copyright © 1999 by Tyrone Geter
All rights reserved.
Published in Canada by Fitzhenry & Whiteside Ltd.,195 Allstate Parkway, Markham, Ontario L3R 4T8.

Library of Congress Cataloging-in-Publication Data
Johnson, Dinah. Sunday week / Dinah Johnson; illustrated by Tyrone Geter.
Summary: Describes the activities that a community of people engage in all week long as they wait
for Sunday, the best day of all. [1. Sunday—Fiction. 2. City and town life—Fiction. 3. Days—Fiction.
4. Afro-Americans—Fiction. 5. Christian life—Fiction.] I. Geter, Tyrone, ill. II. Title.
PZ7.J631634Co 1998 [E]—dc21 97-38298

ISBN 0-8050-4911-8 / First Edition—1999 / Typography by Meredith Baldwin
Printed in the United States of America on acid-free paper. ∞
10 9 8 7 6 5 4 3 2 1
The artist used charcoal and pastels on colored paper to create the illustrations for this book.